A Note to Parents and Caregivers:

Read-it! Joke Books are for children who are moving ahead on the amazing road to reading. These fun books support the acquisition and extension of reading skills as well as a love of books.

Published by the same company that produces *Read-it!* Readers, these books introduce the question/answer and dialogue patterns that help children expand their thinking about language structure and book formats.

When sharing joke books with a child, read in short stretches. Pause often to talk about the pictures and the meaning of the jokes. The question/answer and dialogue formats work well for this purpose. Have the child turn the pages and point to the pictures and familiar words. When you read the jokes, have fun creating the voices of characters or emphasizing some important words. And be sure to reread favorite jokes.

There is no right or wrong way to share books with children. Find time to read with your child, and pass on the legacy of literacy.

Adria F. Klein, Ph.D.
Professor Emeritus
California State University
San Bernardino, California

Managing Editor: Bob Temple
Creative Director: Terri Foley
Editor: Peggy Henrikson
Editorial Adviser: Andrea Cascardi
Designer: Amy Muehlenhardt
Page production: Picture Window Books
The illustrations in this book were prepared digitally.

Picture Window Books
5115 Excelsior Boulevard
Suite 232
Minneapolis, MN 55416
1-877-845-8392
www.picturewindowbooks.com

Printed in the United States of America.

Library of Congress Cataloging-in-Publication Data
Dahl, Michael.
Teacher says / written by Michael Dahl ; illustrated by Ryan Haugen.
p. cm. — (Read-it! joke books)
Summary: A collection of jokes and riddles about teachers, including,
"Why did the student eat her spelling test? Because the teacher said
it was a piece of cake."
ISBN 1-4048-0301-7
1. Schools—Juvenile humor. 2. Education—Juvenile humor. 3. Teachers—
Juvenile humor. 4. Wit and humor, Juvenile. [1. Teachers—Wit and humor.
2. Schools—Wit and humor. 3. Jokes. 4. Riddles.] I. Haugen, Ryan, ill.
II. Title.
PN6231.S3 D35 2004
818'.5402—dc22

2003016669

Teacher Says

A Book of Teacher Jokes

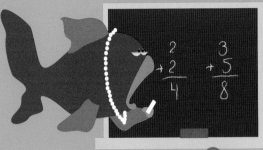

Michael Dahl • Illustrated by Ryan Haugen

Reading Advisers:
Adria F. Klein, Ph.D.
Professor Emeritus, California State University
San Bernardino, California

Susan Kesselring, M.A., Literacy Educator
Rosemount-Apple Valley-Eagan (Minnesota) School District

PICTURE WINDOW BOOKS
Minneapolis, Minnesota

Teacher: "Jason, can you find Australia on the map?"
Jason: "There it is."

Teacher: "Now, Brenda,
    who discovered Australia?"
Brenda: "Jason did!"

Teacher: "I wish you would pay a little attention."

Craig: "I'm paying as little as I can!"

Why was the fish teacher so tired?

Because fish spend
all their time in schools.

Why didn't the little pigs listen to their teacher?

Because he was a big boar! 9

Debbie: "Teacher, would you punish me for something I didn't do?"

Teacher: "Of course not."

Debbie: "Good, because I didn't do my homework."

Teacher: "This looks like your mother's handwriting on your homework."

Scott: "That's because I used her pen."

Dad: "Well, son, how are
   your grades?"
Son: "Underwater."
Dad: "What do you mean?"

Son: "The teacher said they
were below C level."

13

Teacher: "You missed school yesterday."

Rick: "Not very much."

Teacher: "I hope I didn't just catch you cheating on your test."

Tom: "I hope you didn't either."

Teacher: "Dustin, if you had six candy bars on your desk and Eric took two, what would you have?"

Dustin: "A fight."   17

Teacher: "If you add 37,428 and 68,329, divide the answer by 4, then multiply by 6, what do you get?"

Jill: "The wrong answer."

Teacher: "Kathie, why do you have cotton balls in your ears?"

Kathie: "Well, you keep telling me things go in one ear and out the other. I'm just trying to keep everything in."

20

Mom: "Your teacher said you're at the bottom of the class."

Son: "Don't worry. They teach the same thing at both ends."

Teacher: "Johnny, I told you to go to the end of the line."

Johnny: "I tried, but somebody
was already standing there." 23

Why did the student eat her spelling test?

Because the teacher said it was a piece of cake.